Love Grounds and Coffee Poems

by

Todd
&
Deborah Bauer

PublishAmerica
Baltimore

© 2008 by Todd and Deborah Bauer.
All rights reserved. No part of this book may be reproduced, stored in a retrieval system or transmitted in any form or by any means without the prior written permission of the publishers, except by a reviewer who may quote brief passages in a review to be printed in a newspaper, magazine or journal.

First printing

PublishAmerica has allowed this work to remain exactly as the author intended, verbatim, without editorial input.

ISBN: 1-60474-738-2
PUBLISHED BY PUBLISHAMERICA, LLLP
www.publishamerica.com
Baltimore

Printed in the United States of America

*Love Grounds
and
Coffee Poems*

You showed up at the wrong coffee shop;
Or was it me?
I was willing to not meet at all.
OK, fine, we'll try again.
Notice you don't offer to pay for my drink.
OK, fine. I'll pay for it myself.
After all, this is no biggy.
Yes, I know I made you laugh.
I make most people laugh.
You seemed like the others;
Shorter, though. Brighter.
And I liked what we talked about
And something in your eyes
When you talked about art like your lover.
I got hung up on your mouth.
Wanted to feel its wetness on my…
I liked that you made ME laugh,
And you invited me to see your place,
I thought, OK, fine,
I can go over there and see what that's all about.
Just to see.
And then I saw your place,
And the soapstone sculpture,
And you screaming from the walls
And the pain at your core from another time,
But not too far away.
OK, fine. I can hug you.
And then I felt you—from the inside out.
The rest is history.

I met her
at a coffee shop.
She was taller,
more outspoken
and better looking
than I'd thought she'd be.

We talked about the past,
specifically;
and relationships, generally.

She thought,
"What might he look like
with shorter hair?"
And I thought,
"What would she look like
with fewer clothes?"

*When I read mysteries—
Sometimes I like to sneak a peak
At the end…
Because I can t wait,
And the suspense is killing me—
Like now,
With you…*

Half a century
Hasn't crumbled
Her beautifully
Sculpted
Ass.

My hands
Involuntarily
Clench,
Thinking to grasp
That perfect pair.

I didn't want to get close to you at first

Because of a very full plate.

Didn't want to add anything to it—

Especially another man

Now, you're the only one on it.

Damn!

In many past lives
I've ridden a white charger,
wearing the accouterments
of a rescuer.

In this life,
every attempt to
rescue an unfair damsel
has ended with my bitter failure.

Now, one comes who
needs no rescuer.
What am I to do?

*I am used to an aching heart.
When I wake up with a yearning
To be somewhere else
And with someone else,
And maybe be someone else….again.
With you, there is no ache…
Just a light tether drawing me to you;
Willingly, fully present.*

There's no "parting is such sweet sorrow" bullshit,
just a grateful glowing from togetherness.

I had to endure the long draught
before fully drenching myself in the waterfall.

The toy soldier marches in place
and the trapped light strains to escape
the dark vortex.

*You curl around me
in the dark
like a warm overcoat,
offered to share -
or a river flowing between stones
touching water to rock on all points
or like a fine nesting of fitted wooden bowls.
My rump backed into your belly;
your right hand cupping my breast;
my everywhere hair tousled between us
and I feel you drift away,
painting as you go with involuntary twitches
into slumber.
Last night, you went alone
while I shared your heart,
waiting for the dawn.*

We took the night off,
and tomorrow, too. Details
need attending.

I thought I had much
to do, but
all I did was
think of you...

and now I've eaten
another piece of your
pumpkin pie, and wonder
if you miss me like
I do you?

*Soft as spring rains dance,
You kiss me from the inside out—
Suspended in air like hummingbird's flight
Breath and flesh alive to touch.
We pause in the stillness of the night
Open hands between us both,
softly holding the extension of one another's dreams.
You grow on me like the sleepy dawn
As your words restore my deepest heart,
And I hear you.*

My pie-baking babe,
feeds my spirit
and knows me better
than most—
me included;
gives me breathing room
before I know I need it;
insists on hugs and
knows I need it, too;
spends nights warming
my chi with her behind;
assaults me with smiles
and breaks down the walls
to let the light out.

*As close
As we are…
Nothing
Lies between.*

*Another marking of the passing days;
Another marking on my eager skin;
I lift my glass to you
And make you pies
That you devour,
Not unlike the devouring of me—
With light all around,
In the center of our universe;
All things, brand new.*

Staring off
I feel her eyes on me...
studying, memorizing, scrutinizing.

I interrupt her gaze
and she blushes like a guilty school girl.

I haven't done anything
to deserve admiration;
yet, by just being, I've touched her,
and left my mark—
And she, with me.

After you leave,
Your imprint on my space
(Now somewhat shared;
somewhat familiar),
Lingers past the smell of coffee,
The still-wet tub,
And the brutally bruised sheets
Now lying still in the morning sun.

My bed is conspicuously
empty tonight...

your sherbet-colored night shirt
crumpled atop my pile of bathrobes...

the smell of your hair
comes from one of my pillows...

it hasn't been a whole day since I
last saw you...

or a whole hour since I
last spoke to you...

or a whole minute since I
last thought of you.

Up at the crack of noon
Coffee starts to brew
Wild bed hair and bare feet
Robe wrapped
Day warriors
Letting the sun get a head start
Before venturing out into the
Clear day.

Morning Coffee,
And everywhere hair:
Sharing both,
And all things metaphysical
With you.

Each time we talk,
You say things that bring me in…
A little at a time,
Like gathering Calla lilies in the woods…
Pure white;
Like sharing folding sheets.
And vanilla ice cream
And the things I love are softening me;
Opening me like a flower—
Like the opening of my legs for you—
And you bury yourself in my bouquet of embracing limbs—
And I bring you in.

Broken pumpkins underfoot
Like past aspirations
And relationships...

Traversing carefully
So as not to slip in the pulp and spilled seeds
Or step into an old one...

The crisp autumn air
Ripens your cheeks
And I hold your hand.

*Would that you always see me
Through the eyes of a lover—
Every nook, cranny and gentle slope
From my neck to the curve of my heel
And the top of my head to the back of my knee,
Would that you caress me as you do now.
I am past the time of centerfolds and airbrushed perfection;
Past the time of inexperienced coupling.
Yet, I still ravish relentlessly with great abandon;
Fiercely saturated with you—
Even more passionate; Steamingly sensual
Confident and secure in my
Sharing secrets and treasure wherever
We happen to play.
My years on this planet are
Entertwined with my carnal self,
Living my life and breathing—
This body is still my temple and
Not my prison…*

Morning encroaching on noon
and a cup of steaming stimulation
Between my hands.
Cascading covers cover our cuddling.
We coo nonsense and blowing giggles to one another
Like six month olds,
Growing younger;
Together,
One awakening at a time.

*I shook off sleep this morning
Lurching to find you…
After I heard the leather of your jacket
Signal time to go.
You stood up to fold around me
Like a hand cradling a small bird…
Kissing my forehead
As I poured myself to fit against you.
"I'm taller than you," you said.
"I like it," you continued.
"So do I," I said,
"Guess you'll have to wear your boots to bed."
You laughed and held me tighter;
I sighed and let you go.*

Post-coital banter
about who has to pee?
and
are we doing anything tomorrow?
But the big love
cuddles between the lines.

Painting

*You push me into painting
Like off a high dive;
Plummeting with cannonball grace
Into the giddy world of
stretched canvas and brushes;
Tubes of color beckon like forbidden fruit
And multi-faceted rainbows
Splash themselves like music
heard for the first time
across my mind.*

I painted coffee rings
to prove to myself and show the world
that I had achieved psychic unity;
and then,
you showed me how
fragmented
I still am...

*Fanciful, warmly scented,
White terry cloth wrapped;
I lie under an Indian throw…
Still…
Hum of the refrigerator
Almost covers the dedicated rain.
He sleeps beside me
In the next room
Awaiting my sweet transition into dreaming.
Still,
New comfort salves old wounds
Our loving only lifts each other
Towards the graceful day.
Clear eyes pool drops of rain.
Still,
We love.*

Beating my head
Against canvas
Trying to paint my
Salvation;
And the entire
Time she was
Sleeping
Next to me.

If I could give you even a piece of a star;
The part careening into the yet-thin air
From its dark and silent passages—
Now blazing colors,
Much like your coffee rings,
Metamorphosing from a
Quiet imprint on nondescript pages;
Too bright,
Only to be emboldened like the night sky
When the shattering mix of your own heart
And sweeping paint strokes and colors
Enliven your canvas
To calm your restless eye.

(This is a mnemonic poem
about how Deb awoke laughing from a dream,
stumbled into the kitchen with half-closed eyes
and flung out a poorly aimed arm
to receive a glass of morning shake—
splashing it everywhere!)

        Waking
        Walking
        Giggling
        Spilling
        Morning.

Contented calm
Like seeing a full garden
in July.
Burgeoning green richness
As bugs eye the bounty.
Warm sun slows senses
And time stops
When I look into your eyes.

Crisp as dried leaves
Sharp as bare branches;
Autumn's melancholy
Is blunted by you.

I am not known for my patience.
There are buttons under my skin that
Seem to have been implanted
Without my knowing.
Doesn't matter who pushes them.
It's all the same unleashing;
The same automatic program
Will run for one and all who finds the trigger,
And I can't find the off switch before
The extemporaneous exhibit explodes.

This shadow me,
Raging inside like a nefarious ferrel cat;
Indignation over losing control—
Showing inappropriate evidence of the rotting remains—
Shame that those closest to me
Should see this wounded expression I can't yet stop
I feel far too naked to expose
This internal destitution,
And I am far too needy to be brave.

Instead of pulling
The thorn from your foot,
I stuck you with one of my own.
While you wobbled,
You may have tripped over
Something in my unconscious;
Something dark, vicious and
Possessing sharp teeth.

In a bristling instant,
The thing lashed at you
Without my conscious consent.

Crisp fall Sunday afternoon
Art library smells of books
your leather jacket squeaks
as pages turn and you sigh.
Bare branches,
Warm gold leaves,
Blue sky pale
just beyond the window's pane
we sit together
Reading quietly.
I wait for recess!

You're like
Soft new pine needles;
Clouds skipping across a gem-like sky;
A babies soft skin;
The rustling aspen leaves in a gentle spring breeze;
The sweetest sparkling cider.

What I feel for you is
Sharp like cheddar;
Deep like Jung;
Epic like Frodo;
Transformative like Art;
All encompassing like a Circle.

Wordless;
Like the heron
Poised before the setting sun;
Like the chilled snow
Dropping indecisively.
You leave me discomposed;
Enfolding me
Among your dreams of roses
And I,
Who usually speak plenty
Have each breath surrounded by the silence of
"It is enough."

I covertly watch you
Searching for the ever-elusive car keys,
Or the magically disappearing reading glasses
(now crouching in your everywhere hair).

I anxiously observe as you
Gingerly peel my façade
Like a spotted, ripe banana
(revealing the authentic me).

*You give me what I've always wanted.
The small things…
More precious than money in the bank
Or shallow capacity for love.
You have coaxed my heart to open
Like uncurling fingers around the master key
To secret places never shared.
But now, all things, shared with you.*

In your absence,
Bedtime is void of significance,
Home is just a place,
And life is a monotonous maze
Once again.

Sunday Brunch Time

Raining again and still drinking coffee.
Lazing under mounds of warm covers
Surrounded by piles of books—
You open one by Bukowski
And your deep voice begins to tell the story
Of another time in another rain;
Ladies waiting in dimly lit rooms
And the men who visit them by the hour;
Drunken, used up men with shriveled dreams,
Betting on the ponies and
Tired, hardened women, looking for truth in a bottle;
Still betting on love.
Bukowski lost everything but words, you know....
We drift on our raft, dreaming, far away
From the pelting rain just outside the window
Finding your smile as the first thing I see when I open my eyes,
Then Bukowski's words—
Slice to the bone.

I had imbibed Bukowski
And found him bitter in my mouth
But sweet in my soul.

She and I hesitantly exchange poems
And caress each other with our
Written words.

I introduce her to Bukowski,
Serving him with Sunday morning coffee
On last nights sheets;

His blunt words
The shadows
To our shared light.

*We're getting in pretty deep—
I can tell because of my constant, silly grin
Caught in my reflection when I walk by
And how you're on my mind pretty much all the time.
We're getting in pretty deep
Sliding into love like a vat of chocolate pudding
You, who named the TV remote after me
And moved into my well-ordered space—
Bringing tall black bookcases
Full of books on swords, art history, and Carl Jung.
Trudging in your neatly packaged life in
mysterious boxes—
My tall white bookcases, full of books on health,
self-help, real estate
and Kevin Trudeau's Mega Memory—
which I forgot to open,
Look on dubiously from their positions along the wall.
Yin and Yang book cases, I giggle…
Who knew?*

We make love and grow closer.
We sleep to heal
From our wounded pasts.

We shed our histories
To live in this present.

First Night All Moved In

*I could say that my dreams
Are coming true;
The ones where I have a lighthearted mate
Beside me with his shoes in my closet
And his breathing softly
Reminding me that
I have a man in bed—
And I am home, finally, with him…
And he lives here now and I can't just
Get up and drive home for a good night's sleep.
Grinning in the dark as I realize that
He can't just get up and
Drive home, either…*

As you deeply sleep
Beside me
I dream of our lives
Entwining.
Possibilities open
Like wildflowers
in the meadow
Of tomorrow.

I am all over you
From below and above;
Peppering you with kisses.
Wrestling around like kids
"Badger, badger, badger," you say.
I bolster, beckon and bounce
You grin, giggle and grunt.
"Uncle, uncle," you say!
You reach past me to turn out the light
While you "try" to escape…
Of course, I chase you until you catch me

I want to take you
To the museum and show you my favorite paintings,
Like opening a scrapbook showing where I've been.

I want to convey to you
all I think I know about painting
and see what you create with it.

I want to find out
Who I am when I'm part of our couple-ness,
And can't wait for you to tease it out of me.

I swore I wouldn't marry again...

But you have me
Reconsidering that proclamation, just like I've retracted
My aversion to salads or classical violin (which you play
so movingly).

Escalating into love
With you has turned my bitter world upside down.
You fill my half-empty bucket.

Wedding Vows

We said, "I do."
In front of family and friends
You looked wonderful;
Radiant,
Smiling and sweet,
Good enough to…
Well, cake and treats would have to do.

We offer vows
Where I usually stand to paint,
Surrounded by our families
And my offspring of paintings
On a clear Fall day.

Just over a year ago,
We met for coffee.
Now we meet to commit
To a lifetime together.